The Starlight Bride

A Tale of Love and Miracles
Written and Illustrated
by
Paul Owen Lewis

Published by:
Beyond Words Publishing, Inc.
Pumpkin Ridge Road
Route 3, Box 492 B
Hillsboro, OR 97123
Phone: (503) 647-5109
Toll free: (800) 284-9673

Printed in the United States of America
by Dynagraphics, Inc., Portland, Oregon

First Printing: December 1988

ISBN: 0-941831-25-6

For information about a school lecture and
slide show of Starlight Bride, please contact
Beyond Words Publishing.

For RuthAnn & her grandchildren.

To my Starlight Bride.

With thanks to Steve and
Jerene R. for dreams,
for sanctuary.

Once, long ago, in the days of chivalry and honor, there lived a certain King with his Queen and their beloved son.

Now the King had grown old and the time had come to pass the reign of the realm to his son, the Prince.

The King called his son to his side and said:

"My son, Prince of the realm and future King, your mother and I are now old and full of years, and it is time for you to choose a wife — as the law requires of you — and become King in the land after me."

As soon as the King finished speaking to his son, he called for his royal emissaries to mount their horses and assemble at the castle gate.

Said the King to them:

"Go now into all the surrounding realms; to the castles of Kings and Queens, and the manors of Noblemen; and tell them that I, the King in this good land, am about to give the Kingdom to my son, the Prince. But, before I may do this, my son the Prince must first take a wife as our law requires.

"Therefore, I invite any eligible ladies of noble birth who so desire it, to journey to our good land and stay the month of Advent to seek the Prince's favor in this matter. For on the last Sunday of Advent, the Prince shall choose his Queen from among those attending, and marry her, his bride, on Christmas Eve.

"Furthermore, for her comfort, a house shall be built for each lady and her retainers after the style of her own domains."

At once the emissaries rode away and soon returned with the names of the noble ladies who had promised to attend. They also brought with them the plans for the houses to be built. The market in the center of the village was cleared away, and the houses, each of differing appearance, rose quickly around the great tree there.

That first Sunday a great feast of welcome was given in the ladies' honor. The Prince then and there introduced himself to each of the ladies. To his surprise, he found them *all* most charming and beautiful, full of wit and grace. Nothing could be better, or so he thought.

And so it was that over the course of the next two weeks the Prince was very busy. He took tea, danced, sang, enjoyed falconry and long rides in the crisp December air with each of the ladies in turn — until only one day remained before he had to choose.

That very day the Prince went to his father the King and said: "Father, I am greatly troubled. Though I have well acquainted myself with all the good ladies; have danced, sung and enjoyed games of the field with all in turn; I yet *cannot* choose from among them! My heart will not and cannot set one apart from the others."

Well, the King, being old, wise, and familiar with the ways of the heart, replied: "Perhaps, my son, it is because you have measured them by your notions and not *theirs*. For to recognize love, one must know the heart and see beyond the songs and games."

"But father, how can I now see into their hearts with so little time before I must choose?"

Well, the King thought and finally replied: "Tomorrow, we will hold a festival of gifts. Let us invite each of the ladies to prepare and present to you a gift of herself — something from the very heart. Then you shall see."

As soon as the Prince agreed to this, the King sent his royal messengers to announce the festival and have the preparations made.

That night, the Prince could not sleep. He lay tossing and turning, wondering, "What if all the gifts please me equally and I still cannot choose?"

Some time later, he found himself silently climbing the spiral staircase of the castle's highest tower. He entered the small room at the top and knelt at the only window. It looked upon the village below. He could see everything: the houses, the cathedral, the great tree, all under the silent blanket of night.

And he began to pray:

"Dear Lord, I am in great need. I must choose my Queen wisely so that I may rule the Kingdom well as I wish to do. Therefore, I pray thee, help me to know her, the one you have chosen, by granting me a sign. As she stands before me tomorrow, cause the crystal star to shine brightly atop the great tree. In this way will I know your will and obey. Amen."

The day dawned and the festival began. The Prince sat on a small stage in front of the great tree with his father the King and mother the Queen on either side.

As each of the ladies came forward, the Prince glanced behind and upwards at the star to see if it was shining.

Some gave poems, paintings, songs and music, composed just for the Prince. Others gave beautiful tapestries, weavings, delicious cakes and pies. Until, at last, it appeared there were no more presenters.

The star had not shined!

The Prince quickly asked the royal list-keeper if any had not come forward. No, all had.

Greatly alarmed, the Prince looked to his father the King and whispered: "Father, I *yet* cannot choose."

"But my son," said the King, "you *must*! These good ladies and the people have been through much excitement and anticipation. You have had these two weeks and this festival besides — what more do you require?"

"I do not know. Please, I beg of thee, tell them I shall make my decision by tomorrow."

Well, the King, being old, wise and quick with the tongue, stood and said in a loud voice:

"Good ladies, we thank you! Your gifts overwhelm us. In the face of so many wonders displayed, how can one choose so quickly from among them? For to choose this moment would now seem rash indeed. Therefore, the Queen and I ask that my son the

Prince may have the evening to consider your gracious efforts — for he does not wish to overlook any. Let us gather here again tomorrow at this time. Then shall the Prince be better able to make a fitting choice."

To this the ladies agreed, for they too saw the wisdom in this. So, the festival was adjourned.

That night, when all were fast asleep, the Prince again climbed the highest tower and knelt at the window of the chamber. Great tears welled in his eyes and his heart was heavy. He cried aloud:

"Oh Lord, why have you forsaken me in my time of greatest need? For the star did not shine! What am I to do now? They are all waiting for my decision."

Then, to his wonder and amazement, he saw through his tears, far below him, the star atop the great tree shining brightly in the night. And he beheld what appeared to be the figure of a young woman, kneeling at the foot of the tree. He kept silent and watched. Soon, the small dark figure rose, walked away from the tree and vanished between the row of houses on the opposite side of the village. And as she rose and walked away — the star dimmed and then darkened altogether.

"My beloved is here!" cried the Prince.

Down the spiral staircase, through great arched halls and out the castle gate ran the Prince in slippered feet. Standing alone in the village under the great tree, the Prince looked at the houses. All were dark. All were silent. Quickly and quietly he searched each and every window hoping for some sign of the young woman. A single candle, a whispered voice perhaps. He saw and heard nothing.

Early in the morning the Prince went to his father the King and said:

"Beloved father, I have wrestled the night's passing in thought and prayer and am confident I can now make a wise choice. But to do so — I require one more day. Please, I pray thee, grant me this."

Well, the King, being old, wise, and exceedingly patient with his only son, the Prince, agreed to his request. The King then sent his royal emissaries to plead with the ladies for one day more. Though met with displeasure, the emissaries nevertheless returned to the King with the news that all had agreed to one day more for the Prince. For the ladies had seen that to lose all for one day's patience would indeed be foolish.

That night, when all were fast asleep, the Prince once again climbed the high tower and knelt at the chamber window. And he watched. Sure enough, after a short time had passed, he saw the small, dark figure of a young woman appear from between the houses on the opposite side of the village. She approached the tree as before, fell to her knees — and the star began to glow, and became so brilliant that it shined as the brightest star in the sky.

The Prince lost no time. Down the spiral staircase, through the great arched halls and out the castle gate he ran. But, when he arrived in the village, the star was no longer shining. The young woman had vanished as she had the night before. And once again, the Prince searched for a sign of her presence. He again found nothing.

Early in the morning, the Prince again went to his father, the King, and said: "My beloved father and my gracious King, I beg your forgiveness and patience with me for I had not foreseen this. Though I am more confident than ever I can make the best of all possible choices — I find I must have one more day. Please, I pray thee, I beg thee, grant me this. I will not fail you."

Well, even though the King was old, wise, and had seen and heard many strange things in his many years, this was more than even he could understand, for tomorrow was Christmas Eve — the very day of the wedding.

Nevertheless, the good King agreed to his son's request. This time, the King himself visited each of the ladies in turn and begged their patience on his very knees. The ladies agreed to wait.

That night, when all were fast asleep, the Prince did not climb the tower. He instead stole into the village and climbed some ten feet up the great tree and hid himself there among the branches. And he waited. Sure enough, after a short time had passed, he saw the dark figure of the woman approaching from between two houses, as if from the cathedral behind. At the foot of the tree she knelt as before. Suddenly, shafts of soft starlight lit on his shoulders and played on the branches all around him. And the young woman began to pray:

"Dear Lord, our beloved Prince is in great need. He must choose his Queen wisely so that he may rule the Kingdom well as he wishes to do. As *you* will him to do. Therefore, I pray thee, this very evening, help him to know her, the one you have chosen. For myself, dear Lord, I pray, grant me a sign that you have answered my prayer. I shall hide this rose in a tuft of grass here under the tree. Should it be gone in the morning, I shall know that you have granted this. Amen."

The young woman arose and walked away. As she did, the star dimmed and was soon dark altogether.

The Prince lost no time. Down the tree, he took the rose in hand and returned to the castle. That night he dreamt of love.

Early in the morning the Prince again went to his father the King and said: "Father, I have made my decision. Ready the people, for I am about to be married and become their King!"

And so it was that banners were hung and trumpets sounded and all the people assembled in the village around the great tree. Each of the noble ladies wore her finest gown. Each was breathtaking to behold. And each was anxious to know if she would be chosen to be Queen.

By and by all was ready, all was quiet. The Prince stood high on the stage so all might see his certainty in his eyes and hear it in his voice. Now, pulling the rose from his robe, he said in a loud and regal tone:

"Will she who placed this rose at the foot of the great tree last night please come forward."

At this the people began to murmur and ask, "What does he mean? Was this one of the gifts?" The noble ladies looked among themselves to see which of them had done it. No one came forward, and it seemed that none claimed the rose.

Then, a young peasant woman came forward from among the crowd of townspeople. With head bowed low she said in a clear, bright voice:

"It was I, your highness. I placed the rose at the foot of the tree."

The Prince lifted her eyes to his — and he beheld the most beautiful maiden he had ever seen. And his heart was filled with love for her.

Turning to the crowd, he said, "This is she, the one whom I have chosen to be my bride and Queen!"

And having said this the Prince then explained the happenings of the past three nights. The shining star, the identical prayers, and the sign of the rose.

And all agreed this was the work of heaven.

And all rejoiced with the Prince.

One of the court officials then stepped forward and exclaimed:

"But your highness, you cannot marry a commoner, for the law forbids it."

And it was true.

The Prince, the King and Queen, the people, and even the noble ladies themselves were lost in sorrow at the realization.

Then another man stepped forward and said:

"Good people, listen to me! You know me as the caretaker of the cathedral, and this young woman as my daughter who tends the rose garden behind. But, all is not as it appears.

"Many years ago, while travelling the realms beyond the borders of this good Kingdom, I saw from a forest a castle in flames on a hill, besieged by a hostile army. A man, in royal garb and bloodied as if from battle, approached me with a bundle in his arms. He handed me the bundle and begged me to flee — for it contained a child. As I reached to take hold of the child, a bow shot sounded in the forest. The man fell dead at my feet, an arrow through his heart. I escaped with the child and came to settle here in your good Kingdom as caretaker. Later, I found that the child bore a locket around her neck, and upon opening the locket found that she was a Princess, none other than the daughter of the fallen King whose castle was destroyed that day. Look for yourselves at the locket she wears, and see if it is not so!"

They did.

And it was.

So the Prince and Princess were married then and there that Christmas Eve under the great tree. And as they spoke their vows to one another, the crystal star atop the tree shined brightly.